Timber!

Freddie pushed open the door of the workroom. Inside it was dark and spooky-looking.

Freddie saw a tall display case. The beautiful old fire wagon was sitting on the top shelf. But it was too high for him to reach it.

Just as Freddie turned to look for a chair, someone shot out from behind the cabinet and came rushing at him. The person slammed into the cabinet and ran to the open door.

Before Freddie could see who it was, he heard a loud creaking sound.

He turned in time to see the huge cabinet tipping over—falling straight at him!

Books in The New Bobbsey Twins series

Available from MINSTREL Books

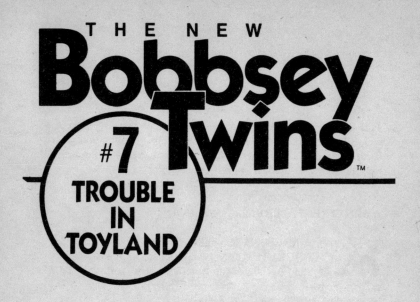

THE NEW Bobbsey Twins

#7 Twins

TROUBLE IN TOYLAND

LAURA LEE HOPE

ILLUSTRATED BY PAUL JENNIS

A MINSTREL® BOOK

PUBLISHED BY POCKET BOOKS

New York   London   Toronto   Sydney   Tokyo   Singapore

This novel is a work of fiction. Names, characters, places and incidents are either the product of the author's imagination or are used fictitiously. Any resemblance to actual events or locales or persons, living or dead, is entirely coincidental.

A MINSTREL PAPERBACK *ORIGINAL*

A Minstrel Book published by
POCKET BOOKS, a division of Simon & Schuster Inc.
1230 Avenue of the Americas, New York, NY 10020

ISBN: 0-671-62658-2

First Minstrel Books printing August, 1988

10 9 8 7 6 5 4 3 2

THE BOBBSEY TWINS, A MINSTREL BOOK and colophon are
registered trademarks of Simon & Schuster Inc.

THE NEW BOBBSEY TWINS is a trademark of
Simon & Schuster Inc.

Printed in the U.S.A.

Contents

TROUBLE
IN
TOYLAND

1

Trouble in Toyland

"We're almost there!" Flossie Bobbsey said eagerly. "It's the biggest toy store in Lakeport."

Flossie stared out the window of the family station wagon.

"So what?" Freddie muttered. He and Flossie were twins. They both had blond hair and blue eyes.

"Come on, Freddie." Flossie gave her brother her biggest smile. "It'll be fun. And Jillian said she'd show me all the new dolls."

"So why do I have to go with you?" Freddie asked. He leaned back in his seat and folded his arms.

"I bet she'll even show you the newest video games," Flossie said.

Mrs. Bobbsey smiled as she drove through Lakeport's downtown shopping area. She felt sure Freddie was one of a kind—the only boy who *didn't* want to visit a toy store.

"Think about it, Freddie," said Bert Bobbsey. He was curled up in the back of the car, reading the latest Rex Sleuther detective manual. Rex was Bert's favorite fictional hero. "We've been invited to play in a toy store. It sure won't be boring."

"Yeah, but 'Jinx' Jenkins invited us!" Freddie said.

"Jillian Jenkins is not a jinx!" Flossie insisted.

"Oh, yeah?" Freddie turned to face her. "What about when my lunch spilled all over me? And when I sat on that wet painting in class? And—"

"Those were accidents," said Flossie.

"No they weren't," Freddie said. "Jillian's always around when something goes wrong."

"All right, you two," said Mrs. Bobbsey. "That's enough arguing for one day."

The two children grumbled as they settled back in their seats.

Nan Bobbsey, Bert's twin, was sitting in the front seat.

She and Bert were twelve years old. They had dark brown hair and brown eyes.

Nan looked up from a sketch she'd been working on. "Don't worry, Mom. Freddie'll be fine when he sees the new Star Ranger space cruiser."

"You mean they've got—" Freddie caught himself. He turned to see Flossie grinning at him. "Big deal," Freddie said.

"Freddie, I'm writing a story on the owner of the store, Mr. Tobias Jenkins," said Mrs. Bobbsey. She was a part-time reporter for the *Lakeport News.* "He's a man who loves toys and children very much. You might enjoy yourself."

"Is the story about the opening of his new toy museum?" Nan asked.

"That's right," said Mrs. Bobbsey. "Mr. Jenkins has taken over the old town hall and turned it into a toy museum. The building will be filled with Mr. Jenkins's antique toy collection."

"Antique toys?" Freddie leaned forward. "I never saw those at the store."

"You wouldn't have, Freddie," said Mrs. Bobbsey. "Mr. Jenkins collects them for his own enjoyment. They're not for sale. Antique toys are toys that were made years and years ago."

"You mean like when Grandma was a girl?" asked Flossie.

"That's right," said Mrs. Bobbsey. "Mr. Jenkins has hundreds of antique toys. There are colorful carousels as big as our kitchen table. Beautiful music boxes that play many different songs. And even toy cars and airplanes that make sparks as they race across the room."

"See, Freddie?" said Flossie. "Jillian's grandfather has the biggest bunch of toys anywhere. Old and new! We'll have lots of fun at the store."

"Well . . ." Freddie was weakening.

"Great!" Flossie cheered.

"But when things start going wrong—" Freddie said.

"Don't worry. Nothing will go wrong." Flossie was beaming.

"I'm glad that's settled," said Mrs. Bobbsey. "Because here we are."

The station wagon stopped in front of a big white building. The Bobbseys stared at the two large storefront windows. Each one was filled with brightly colored toys and decorations.

Above the revolving door was a large red and gold sign. It read: Welcome to More & More Toys. If it isn't here—it hasn't been made.

The Bobbseys scrambled out of the car as fast as they could.

"Now, don't forget," Mrs. Bobbsey called out. "I'll pick you up in two hours."

"Don't worry, Mom. We'll be right here." Flossie was eager to go inside.

"Fine. I'll see you later." Mrs. Bobbsey waved good-bye. Then she pulled out into the traffic.

The Bobbseys whirled around and raced through the revolving doors. Inside, they were greeted by a wonderful sight. There were toys everywhere they turned.

The first-floor walls were lined with games, dolls, and stuffed animals. The aisles were filled with baseball, hockey, and football gear. There were goofy rubber monsters and racing cars. There was even a wading pool filled with bright blue water.

A large winding staircase led to the second floor. Up there the Bobbseys could see bicycles, space toys, and video games.

"Where should we go first?" Nan asked with excitement.

"I think we should find Jillian," Flossie said.

"Not me." Freddie ran toward a display of small sports cars. "I'm going to try one of these. They're remote controlled."

"I'm with you!" Bert said. He ran to catch up with his brother.

Nan and Flossie followed. They arrived just as Freddie placed one of the cars on the floor.

He picked up the control box and began pressing the buttons. Instantly the car did a series of figure eights and circles.

"This is great!" Freddie cried. "Look, even the lights work."

"And you can control it from up to fifty feet away," said Bert.

Flossie was getting impatient. "I still think we should look for Jillian."

"In a minute," Freddie said. "Look at this." The Bobbseys watched the car circle a display near the end of the aisle.

Freddie was doing fine until someone stepped up behind him and covered his eyes. "Hi, Freddie!" he heard a small voice say.

Freddie whirled around. There stood a pretty little girl. She had brown hair, freckles, and a shy smile.

Freddie wasn't happy to see her. But before he could say anything, Flossie screamed, "Freddie! The car!"

Everyone turned to see the sports car racing down the aisle at top speed.

A customer leapt for safety—and knocked over a display of yellow tennis balls. The balls bounced along the floor. Children happily ran after them, chased by parents and several angry store clerks.

Freddie turned to look at the freckle-faced girl. "Hi, Jillian," he said with a sigh. He gave

Flossie an I–told–you–so look but didn't say a word.

The Bobbseys were about to help pick up the balls, when a voice called out, "What is going on here?"

"It was an accident, Grandpa," Jillian said.

"It's Mr. Jenkins," Flossie whispered to Freddie.

"Oh, great," Freddie groaned. "Now I'm really in for it."

A short elderly man was walking up to them. He had gray hair sticking out in all directions. And he wore a suit that was just a little too big. But his eyes were warm and friendly-looking. The store owner didn't look angry at all.

"I'm sorry," Freddie said as Tobias Jenkins reached them. "The toy car got away."

"So I see," said Mr. Jenkins calmly. "Well, don't worry. The clerks will pick up the balls in no time. But maybe I should take that control box."

Freddie quickly handed the control box to the store owner.

"So," Mr. Jenkins went on, "you must be the Bobbsey twins." The Bobbseys all nodded. "Jillian has told me about you. You children like to solve mysteries." Mr. Jenkins's eyes twinkled.

"We help the police with the real tough ones," Bert said proudly.

"We like mysteries, Mr. Jenkins," said Flossie. "But we like toys too."

"Naturally." Mr. Jenkins chuckled. "Well, then, why don't Jillian and I give you the fifty-cent tour."

The Bobbseys couldn't hide their excitement. Jillian and her grandfather led them all through the store. Nan found a paint set she liked. Bert bought a Rex Sleuther action figure. Freddie tested all the new computer games, and Flossie hugged almost every stuffed animal in sight.

On the upper level, Mr. Jenkins introduced them to the store manager. She was a short woman with a funny little nose. Freddie thought she looked like a mouse.

"This is Miss Celia Penny," said Mr. Jenkins. "Miss Penny, these are the Bobbseys."

The store manager gave them a quick twitching smile. It was so fast, the kids weren't sure they'd seen it.

"She looks awfully nervous," Flossie whispered to Jillian.

"She always looks like that," Jillian whispered back. "And she's been working for Grandpa for a whole year."

"Now," Mr. Jenkins said suddenly, "for the special surprise. Last night I received two beautiful antique toys."

"What are they?" asked Nan.

"A ceramic doll and a horse-drawn fire wagon," Mr. Jenkins said. "They're in my workroom, just down this aisle. Would you like to see them?"

"Sure!" the kids answered.

Mr. Jenkins turned toward Miss Penny. "Celia, you haven't seen them yet, have you?"

"No." Her voice squeaked. "I haven't been in your workroom today."

Mr. Jenkins gestured down the aisle. "Well, then, let's all—"

"I can't, Mr. Jenkins," said Miss Penny. "And the head cashier needs to see you first. She said it's very important." With that, Miss Penny disappeared down an aisle.

Mr. Jenkins frowned. "You children wait right here. I'll be back in a minute."

The Bobbseys and Jillian watched as Mr. Jenkins went down the staircase. Then Flossie insisted they go look at a display of stuffed pink bears.

"I don't want to look at some dumb pink bear," said Freddie as he walked off. He wandered around the aisles.

He stopped now and then to look at the bikes and the new Micro-Man skateboards. He'd just decided to look for the Star Ranger space cruiser, when he saw the door. It was at the end of the aisle, and it was marked Workroom.

"That must be where Mr. Jenkins was going

to take us," Freddie whispered to himself. "Maybe I can get a look at the fire wagon."

The door was slightly open. So Freddie pushed it open farther and peeked inside.

At first Freddie wasn't sure he wanted to go in. Most of the room was in deep shadows, dark and spooky-looking. He found the light switch, but he couldn't reach it.

Freddie's eyes adjusted to the darkness. He saw a tall display case inside the room. It was standing next to a large wooden worktable.

Maybe the fire wagon is in that cabinet, Freddie thought. Slowly, cautiously, he walked into the room.

As he neared the display, Freddie kept looking around. All he could see were faint shapes and shadows. Sometimes the shadows seemed to move.

Finally Freddie reached the display case. He could see the fire wagon sitting on the top shelf. But it was too high for him to reach it.

Just as Freddie turned to look for a chair, someone shot out from behind the cabinet and came rushing at him. The person slammed into the cabinet and ran toward the open door.

Before Freddie could see who it was, he heard a loud creaking sound. He turned in time to see the huge cabinet tipping over—falling straight at him!

2

Wagon Trail

The cabinet was falling fast.

Freddie jumped back and slammed into something—Mr. Jenkins's worktable. Quickly Freddie dropped to the floor and rolled under the table—seconds before the huge cabinet crashed to the floor!

He lay there for a moment, afraid to move. Then he heard a familiar voice.

"Freddie! Are you in there?" Nan called.

"Here I am!" Freddie shouted. "Over here!"

He headed for the door by crawling along under the table.

The door swung open. Nan, Bert, Flossie, and Jillian ran into the room. Bert found the switch and turned on the lights.

They saw Freddie crawl out from under the table. Nan was the first to reach him. "Are you all right?"

"I'm okay," Freddie mumbled. He tried to dust himself off.

Nan knew Freddie was a little shaken. As she helped him up she could feel him still trembling.

"Ooooo, Freddie! Look what you did." Flossie was pointing at the wrecked display case.

"I didn't do that," said Freddie. "Someone was in here. They pushed it over when they ran out."

Jillian and the Bobbseys all looked at one another—then back at Freddie.

"It's true," said Freddie. "Don't you believe me?"

Before the kids could answer, Miss Penny rushed into the room. She stopped suddenly when she saw the smashed cabinet.

"What have you children done?" she asked in her high-pitched voice.

All the kids tried answering at the same time. But Flossie's voice topped them all. "Freddie's clumsy, but he didn't mean to break it!"

Miss Penny looked at Freddie with angry, squinting eyes. "Young man, Mr. Jenkins's fire wagon was on the top shelf of that case. You've broken it!" She turned and walked over to the wreckage.

At her feet were pieces of a broken toy. It was a metal horse-drawn fire wagon. It was broken in two, and the horses and wheels were scattered across the room.

"I didn't do it," Freddie said. "Honest."

Just then Tobias Jenkins walked in. He was smiling until he saw the smashed case. "What happened?" he asked.

"It was an accident." Jillian took her grandfather's hand. "The case fell over, but Freddie didn't—"

"The doll is on the worktable," Miss Penny said. "But I'm afraid Freddie has destroyed your wagon."

Nan turned to look at the doll on the worktable. It had a beautiful baby-doll face. The eyes were blue, and they seemed to sparkle. The lips were painted a pretty shade of pink.

Nan was amazed at how real it looked. She was about to say something, when she saw Mr. Jenkins's face.

Nan and all the Bobbseys could see the sadness in his eyes.

Nan reached out and put her hand on Freddie's shoulder. She could tell he didn't know what to say.

"Was anybody hurt?" Mr. Jenkins asked. He sounded really concerned.

"No, sir," Bert answered. He knelt down and picked up a piece of the wagon. "We're real sorry about this."

"And we'll help clean it up," Nan offered.

"No, no. Don't touch any of that glass. You could hurt yourselves."

"We'll just pick up the toy parts," said Flossie. She and Jillian hurried across the room to get the horses.

Freddie stood with his hands in his pockets. He told his story to Mr. Jenkins. But when he finished, he felt the toy-store owner didn't really believe him.

Meanwhile Bert had been examining the underside of the wagon. He asked Nan to give him the piece she was holding. It was the rod that held the horses to the wagon.

"Maybe we can fix this wagon," said Bert. "I can glue these two plastic pieces together."

"Plastic?" The toy man wrinkled his brow. "What plastic pieces? That toy is made entirely of metal. The wagon, horses, and the two firemen."

"Not all of it," Nan said slowly. "This stick is plastic."

"And so is some of the wagon," said Bert. He gave it to Mr. Jenkins.

"You're right," Mr. Jenkins said with alarm. "It's painted to look like metal."

"Is that so bad?" Jillian asked her grandfather. "Lots of kids' toys are plastic."

"But they didn't have plastic when this toy was made," Tobias Jenkins answered.

"Just how old is this toy?" asked Nan.

"If this is the real wagon, it was made in 1875," Mr. Jenkins said. "That makes it over one hundred years old. It's worth thousands of dollars."

Bert let out a low whistle.

"If it's a fake—it's worthless," Mr. Jenkins continued. "Come to my office quickly. I want to look this up in my catalogue."

The children and Miss Penny followed Mr. Jenkins down to the main floor. They went to the back of the store and through a door marked Private.

This was Tobias Jenkins's office. And all around the Bobbseys were stacks of papers and diagrams of toys.

"This room is even messier than yours," Nan whispered to Bert.

Bert gave Nan a half smile. But his attention was on the tall, heavyset man standing in the middle of the room.

"Hubert," said Tobias Jenkins. "What are you doing here?"

"That's Mr. Desmond," Jillian whispered to Freddie. "He sells antiques. You know, stuff that was made a long time ago, like furniture, jewelry, and toys. Mr. Desmond has almost as many old toys as Grandpa."

Mr. Desmond eyed the group of children. He didn't seem pleased to see them. He turned back to Mr. Jenkins to answer his question. "I'm here to make another offer for your toy collection."

"I'm not interested." Mr. Jenkins picked up a book from his desk.

"Tobias." The antiques dealer pulled out his wallet. "Money is no object. I'll pay anything you ask."

"Hubert," said Mr. Jenkins, "I don't want—"

Hubert Desmond held up his hand to stop Mr. Jenkins. "Yes, yes, I know. You love these toys. You love all toys. And you want this museum for the children. I've heard it a thousand times."

"Well, here's a thousand and one." Mr. Jenkins puffed up his chest. "No."

"Everything has a price," said Mr. Desmond.

Tobias Jenkins slammed the book shut. "We'll discuss this at another time, Hubert. Right now I have to call the police."

Everyone in the room was shocked.

"Why are you calling the police?" asked Hubert Desmond.

Mr. Jenkins held up parts of the broken wagon. "When I bought this toy, it was genuine. I checked it, and so did the dealer. All of it was made of solid metal.

"Now, thanks to these children"—Tobias Jenkins pointed at the Bobbseys—"I know this isn't the same toy. This is a fake. I'm afraid the real one is gone.

"It's been stolen."

3
Getting Warmer

It wasn't long before Lieutenant Pike of the Lakeport police arrived.

He came through the office doorway, looking very official. "Good afternoon, Mr. Jenkins. I—" Then he saw the Bobbseys.

"Hello, Lieutenant Pike," Flossie said cheerfully.

Bert, Nan, and Freddie smiled as they saluted the lieutenant.

Lieutenant Pike let out a long sigh and smiled. "Somehow . . . I should have known you'd be here."

The Bobbseys had helped Lieutenant Pike before. They thought he was the best police detective in all of Lakeport.

"Lieutenant," Tobias Jenkins said angrily. "There's a toy thief in Lakeport."

For fifteen minutes Mr. Jenkins and the Bobbseys told their stories. Lieutenant Pike took very careful notes and examined the broken toy.

He even questioned the antiques dealer, Hubert Desmond. Then he asked Celia Penny, the store manager, what she knew. The lieutenant asked when the antique toys arrived at the store. Then he wanted to know how many of Mr. Jenkins's toys had been moved to the museum.

The Bobbseys sat around the room, watching and listening. Nan even drew sketches of everyone. One picture showed Mr. Jenkins ruffling his hair. Another had Celia Penny holding her arms. A third sketch showed Mr. Desmond tugging on his tie.

But when all the questioning was over, Lieutenant Pike didn't look happy. "We'll get right on this, Mr. Jenkins." The lieutenant slipped his notebook into his jacket. "But I have to say—it's not going to be easy."

"Why not?" asked Hubert Desmond.

"Because we have no idea when or where the switch was made. We don't even know why yet."

"I bet the thief was the man in the workshop," said Freddie. "The one who ran out of the room."

"Any customer or employee could have gone in and out of that workroom," said Lieutenant Pike. "We'll check it out, but I can't promise much." A moment later Lieutenant Pike was gone.

Everyone was quiet for a minute. Then Mr. Jenkins looked up from his desk. "I can't understand how this could have happened."

"At least the doll is a real antique," Miss Penny said as she stood up from the couch. "But it's terrible to think someone could have stolen that fire wagon."

"Don't worry," Freddie said. "We'll find the crook."

"That's right," said Bert. "We've solved crimes before. And we'll solve this one too."

Miss Penny gave Bert a quick pat on the head. "That's very sweet, child. But I think you should leave this to the grown-ups."

She walked over to speak with Mr. Jenkins and Mr. Desmond.

"I hate when people do that," Bert mumbled. He gave his hair a quick brush with his fingers.

"They just don't believe we can do it," said Freddie.

"Can you really find out who did this?" asked Jillian.

"We can sure try," said Nan.

"That's right," Bert added. He turned up the collar of his shirt. "From now on—the Bobbseys are on the case."

The following morning was warm and sunny. The Bobbseys sat in their kitchen, eating breakfast and talking about the case.

Mr. and Mrs. Bobbsey couldn't help being amused at some of the things they were hearing.

"I think it's Mr. Desmond," said Flossie. She was drowning her pancakes in strawberry syrup. "He likes money more than anything. Just like Freddie."

"I do not!" Freddie said. "I just save my money better than you."

"Can't you remember anything about the man in Mr. Jenkins's workroom?" Nan asked. She nibbled on some fresh strawberries.

"No," Freddie answered. "But I bet the crook is still around Lakeport. Mr. Jenkins has a lot more toys to steal."

Bert was busily spreading peanut butter over his pancakes. "But why did the crook steal the fire wagon?"

"Because it was kind of nice," answered Freddie. "Even if it didn't run on batteries."

"No!" Flossie exclaimed. "It was for the money! Mr. Jenkins said the real one was worth a lot of money."

Bert nodded slowly. "Yeah . . . but why leave a fake toy behind? That's weird."

"Bert's right," said Nan. "If we knew why the thief left the fake one, maybe we could figure out who he was."

"I don't believe it," said Mr. Bobbsey. "The two of you agreeing on how to solve a crime."

Bert and Nan smiled at each other.

Just then the doorbell rang.

Mrs. Bobbsey went to answer it and returned with a visitor.

"Hello, everybody," Jillian said with a big smile.

"The Jinx," Freddie mumbled. He quickly moved the open syrup bottle away from the edge of the table. But when he pulled his hand back, he flipped his plate up. A stack of syrup-covered pancakes flopped right into his lap, and slid off onto the floor.

Everyone tried not to laugh as Freddie dumped his breakfast into the garbage, then helped himself to more pancakes.

"I wanted you to come to the museum with me," Jillian said to the twins. "Maybe you can

find some clues." She pretended she hadn't seen Freddie's accident. "How about it? Miss Penny is waiting outside to drive us."

"Are you riding in your grandfather's neat old car?" asked Bert.

"Yes," said Jillian. She walked over to the table. "Grandpa says it's an antique too."

"It is," said Mrs. Bobbsey. "It's a limo from the 1930s."

Jillian turned to Mr. and Mrs. Bobbsey. "Is it all right if the twins come with me?" she asked.

"I think so," said Mr. Bobbsey. "Just as soon as Freddie cleans up."

Freddie got up quietly and walked out of the room.

It didn't take long to reach the toy museum.

The two-story red-brick building had once been the town hall. Now Tobias Jenkins was turning it into something for the children. In three days this would be a big antique-toy museum.

As they pulled into the parking lot, a car suddenly cut across their path. Nan turned in time to see that the driver was Hubert Desmond, the antiques dealer.

"He looks pretty angry," said Nan.

"Mr. Jenkins probably turned him down again," said Miss Penny as she parked the car.

"Mr. Desmond isn't used to people saying no to him."

"Come on!" said Flossie. "I can't wait to get inside!"

A few moments later the Bobbseys were standing in the main hall. In front of them were two corridors that led to different exhibits.

"Wow!" said Freddie. "This museum is even bigger than the store!"

"You should see the second floor," said Jillian. "There's more stuff up there."

"Why don't you children look around." Miss Penny nudged them toward one of the rooms. "I promised to check on something for Mr. Jenkins. I'm sure you'll find something to amuse you." She walked off in the opposite direction.

"Where are the dolls?" Flossie asked with excitement.

"This way!" said Jillian.

"But I don't want to see any dolls," Freddie said.

"The electric train set is this way too." Jillian's eyes twinkled.

"Trains!" said Bert and Freddie.

"A whole room of trains! With bridges and tunnels and everything," Jillian said.

"Come on, Freddie." Bert put his arm around Freddie's shoulder. "We can, uh, uh—"

"Look for clues?" Freddie said, smiling.

The two boys raced ahead of the girls and down the corridor.

Soon they reached the connecting door between the doll and train rooms. But just as they were about to enter, Bert grabbed Freddie's arm. "Look," he whispered.

Freddie turned in time to see a man hurry through a side door. He was wearing dirty work clothes and carrying a small box in his arms.

Quickly the boys raced after him. They arrived at the door just as the man stepped into a freight elevator. The doors closed behind him.

"I wonder who that was," said Bert.

"I don't know," Freddie replied. "But that box was just the right size for a toy."

"Like a fire wagon with horses," said Bert. "Come on. Let's ask Jillian where that elevator goes."

The boys ran back to the doll room. They found the girls admiring a beautiful doll sitting behind a toy piano.

"The clothes look so real," said Flossie. She moved closer for a better look. "What does it do?"

"It's mechanical," Jillian explained. "When you turn it on, it plays a song."

"Like a music box," said Nan.

"That's nice," Bert interrupted. "But we just—"

Suddenly they heard a terrible scream.

"That sounds like Miss Penny!" Jillian said.

"Come on!" said Bert.

The kids ran back into the main hall.

"Do you smell something?" asked Nan.

"Smoke!" Bert exclaimed.

"You're right." Flossie looked a little frightened.

Another scream echoed off the walls.

"Up these stairs!" yelled Nan.

The kids raced up the stairs as fast as they could. At the top of the stairs was a long hall with large doorways on either side.

"Look," said Freddie. He pointed to a doorway just down the hall. The room seemed to be filled with flickering yellow and orange lights.

"Let's go," Bert said as they ran down the hall.

The children stopped when they reached the door. The room was filled with smoke. One of the toy displays was on fire. Miss Penny was trying to beat back the blaze with her jacket. But the fire was spreading. Flames were rising toward the ceiling.

In a few minutes the whole room would be on fire!

4

Boxed In

Bert and Nan desperately searched for some way to help Miss Penny. Then Nan spotted a heavy curtain hanging on a nearby window.

"Bert," Nan yelled, "come on!"

The two twins tore down the curtain and ran back to the fire.

"Throw this over the fire!" Bert shouted.

Working hard, Miss Penny and the older Bobbseys threw the heavy cloth onto the burning display. But it wasn't enough. Black smoke rose to the ceiling, and burning embers fell to the floor. If the carpet caught on fire, everything would be destroyed.

Nan called to the younger kids. "Get help! Hurry!"

Freddie whirled around, looking up and down the hallway. In a flash he spotted a small fire extinguisher mounted on the wall. He grabbed it and ran toward the flames. From a safe distance he began spraying the carpet, trying to keep the fire from spreading.

Flossie and Jillian headed for the stairway, screaming as loudly as they could. They hoped they'd find Mr. Jenkins somewhere downstairs. But as they reached the railing, Flossie spotted a small red panel on the wall.

"Jillian!" Flossie pointed at the wall. "The fire alarm! Help me reach it!"

Using all her strength, Jillian lifted Flossie as high as she could. Flossie's little fingers reached up, grabbed the lever, and pulled.

Instantly the fire alarm rang throughout the building. Within seconds Mr. Jenkins arrived with the janitor.

The two men helped battle the flames. Ten minutes later the fire was out.

"I don't know what happened, Mr. Jenkins," Miss Penny said. She rubbed her arms nervously. "I was in here checking the exhibits, when suddenly this one just burst into flames."

Mr. Jenkins looked sad and tired as he stared at the ashes. "Well, they're gone. Totally destroyed."

"What were they?" Nan asked.

"Three teddy bears made over eighty years ago." Tobias Jenkins shook his head. "It took me five years to find them. They had little woolen bodies, leather noses, and glass eyes. They were pretty . . . to me, anyway."

"Mr. Jenkins." Bert was bending over a section of the ashes. "Did this display use electricity?"

"No, it didn't," Mr. Jenkins replied. "Why?"

"Because there's a cord going from that outlet to the ashes." Bert pointed to the wire. "I've read how you can set a fire with an electric cord."

Miss Penny gave Bert a strange look. "I suppose that was in some silly comic book?"

"No, it wasn't," Bert said proudly. "It was in one of my official Rex Sleuther manuals."

"Well," said Mr. Jenkins, "it doesn't matter where you found out about it. You're right. That wire shouldn't be there.

"Maybe I'm the unluckiest man alive. Or someone is out to destroy my collection. Anyway, if this keeps up, Lakeport won't have a toy museum. Not by Saturday morning—or any time soon."

Miss Penny sighed, then headed for the door. "I'll call the police and fire departments, Mr. Jenkins. We need *professionals* to look into this."

Mr. Jenkins turned to the janitor. "Thanks for your help, Pete."

"No problem," said Pete. "I'll come back later and clean up this room."

Bert and Freddie watched as the janitor followed Miss Penny out of the room. They noticed he was the same man they'd seen earlier—the man carrying the small box and hurrying into the elevator. The brothers exchanged a glance.

Nan waited until Miss Penny had left the room. Then she turned to Mr. Jenkins. "We think someone *is* after your collection, Mr. Jenkins."

"That's right," said Bert. "First a robbery, now a fire. It has to be on purpose, Mr. Jenkins. Nobody's that unlucky."

"I am!" Jillian stood near the doorway. Tears were running down her face. "This is all my fault."

"That's dumb, Jillian. And you know it!" Flossie said.

"No, it isn't," Jillian sobbed. "Even before I came to live with Grandpa, things always went wrong. I'm a jinx! All the kids call me that— even Freddie!"

Before anyone could say a word, Jillian ran from the room.

"I'd better find her," said Mr. Jenkins. "I

think she and I need to talk a little." He turned and left the room.

"Let's go find Jillian too," Flossie said. "Maybe we can help her feel better."

"The best way to help everybody is to find the thief," said Nan.

"And to catch the person who set the fire," Freddie added.

"Right," said Bert. "Let's look for more clues before the police get here."

The Bobbseys went to work and searched the entire room. There were other exhibits in there, and some antique toy posters on the walls.

"These toys are wonderful," said Nan. She was standing in front of a display of a cut-out city. "It must have taken forever to paint all these little details."

"Why didn't the crook set fire to any of these things?" Bert wondered out loud.

"Maybe he thought the whole room would burn down," Freddie replied.

Bert wasn't convinced. "First I thought he was stealing the toys for money. But if he burns the toys—then how can he sell them?"

"I don't know," said Nan, shaking her head. "But let's keep looking around."

The kids continued searching. After a while, they gave up.

"Nothing," Bert said with a sigh. "So what do we do now?"

"We split up," Nan replied. "Freddie and I will go home and check Mom's computer. She has notes on Mr. Jenkins and his toy collection."

"Let me work the computer," Freddie said.

"Okay." Nan put a hand on Flossie's shoulder. "And Flossie can stay with Jillian for a while. Try to cheer her up, Floss."

"No problem." Flossie's big blue eyes twinkled.

"Great!" said Bert. "That leaves me free to work on my own."

"To do what?" asked Flossie.

"Find the man Freddie and I saw sneaking into the elevator. That janitor." Bert walked over to the doorway. "And according to my Rex Sleuther manual—it's best to tail a suspect alone."

Two hours later Bert was hiding behind a car across from the museum. Everyone had left except for Pete, the janitor.

From his position Bert could see the front of the building and the alley alongside. If the thief showed up, Bert would know it.

"Rex Sleuther's stakeout rule number sixteen," Bert whispered to himself. "Cover all the exits, and stay alert."

Just then, a large truck pulled into the museum's alley.

The museum door opened, and Pete stepped out to greet the driver. He was carrying the small box Bert had seen earlier.

Pete placed the box in the truck. Then he spoke to the driver. A moment later the two men went inside the building.

Bert dashed across the street. He had to get a look at those boxes. Maybe the men were stealing more of Mr. Jenkins's toy collection.

Bert reached the back of the truck and peeked inside. It was filled from top to bottom with boxes. "Sleuther's rule number thirty-six," Bert muttered. "Be sure of your evidence before you call the cops."

Bert jumped into the truck and began to examine the cargo. The boxes were labeled More & More Toys. Bert tried to find one that was open. Carefully he worked his way deeper and deeper into the truck. But every box was sealed.

Just as he was about to leave, he heard voices. The two men were returning. Bert ducked behind a large box.

"Take 'em away," Bert heard Pete say. "They've been waiting a long time for this load."

"Sure thing," the driver said. "We can take it easy once we get rid of these old toys."

Old toys! Bert thought to himself. I've found the—

Suddenly the back doors slammed shut. The truck's engine roared into life.

Bert hurried to the doors and tried to push them open. "Locked," he whispered.

The truck backed out of the alley and headed up the street.

Bert was trapped. And there wasn't one Rex Sleuther rule that could help him now.

5

Too Many Pieces

It was six o'clock in the evening when the phone rang. Nan jumped up and grabbed the extension in the kitchen.

She and Freddie had been very worried about Bert. They hadn't heard from him in almost four hours.

"Hello?" Nan said anxiously. She paused for a second. "Bert? Bert Bobbsey, where are you!"

"Where is he?" Freddie asked.

"You're where?" Nan exclaimed.

"Where?" Freddie reached for the phone, but Nan pushed his hand away.

"How—? I can't . . ." Nan stammered.

Freddie was getting frustrated. "Can't what? Where is he? Did he find any clues?"

"Freddie!" Nan said sharply. "Wait a minute. All right, Bert. I'll tell Mom when she gets home. Just stay put!" Nan hung up.

"So where is he?" Freddie said, trying to be calm.

"In Amesbury," Nan said.

"Amesbury!" Freddie shouted. "That's an hour away! How'd he get there?"

Nan was about to reply, when the phone rang again. "Hello. Oh, hi, Floss. How are Jillian and Mr. Jenkins?"

Freddie ran into the living room and picked up the extension.

". . . and it's all because of dumb old Freddie," Flossie's voice came over the line.

"Who are you calling dumb?" asked Freddie.

"You." Flossie sounded really angry. "Jillian still thinks she's a jinx because of you."

Freddie dropped down onto the couch. "I'm not the only one who calls her that!"

"All right, all right," said Nan. "Floss, we'll make it up to Jillian as soon as we solve this case. Now, has anything happened over there?"

"Just that nasty Mr. Desmond," Flossie said. "He came here and asked Mr. Jenkins to sell his toys again."

"And Mr. Jenkins said no?" asked Nan.

"That's right." There was a pause. Then Flossie said, "Nan, can I stay for dinner? They're having spaghetti and meatballs."

"I'll ask Mom," Nan said. "Where's Miss Penny?"

"She went home an hour ago." There was another pause. "They're having strawberry ice cream for dessert."

Nan sighed. "Floss, I promise I'll ask Mom." Nan reminded Flossie to keep her eyes open, then said good-bye.

Nan wandered into the living room and began pacing around the room. She didn't look forward to telling her mother where Bert was. Or that they had to go get him.

Meanwhile Freddie had returned to Mrs. Bobbsey's computer. His fingers rapidly worked the keys. In seconds the screen filled with his mother's notes on antique toys.

Freddie read them for the fourth time. He was still amazed at how they used to make toys by hand. And he was surprised at how much some of those toys were worth now. This made him more determined than ever to save every toy he had.

Freddie was about to quote some prices to Nan, when he heard a car pull into their driveway.

"Uh-oh," Nan said softly. "It's Mom."

A few moments later Mrs. Bobbsey walked into the house. "Hi, you two. Did you have a nice day?" She glanced around the room. "Where's Flossie and Bert?"

Nan lowered her head. "Ummm, Mom . . . can we talk?"

When Nan finished explaining, Mrs. Bobbsey was very quiet. She calmly picked up her keys and headed for the car.

Nan and Freddie decided they'd better go with her—for Bert's sake.

Later that evening the whole family gathered in Bert's room. They listened carefully as Bert finished telling his story. "So the driver found me when he opened up the back of the truck. I couldn't tell him I was spying on him—"

"What *did* you tell him?" asked Mr. Bobbsey.

Bert sat on the floor picking at the wool rug. "I said I was just looking around and got locked in. He was pretty mad. He said it was a dangerous thing to do. Then—"

"Yes?" Mrs. Bobbsey said. She sounded annoyed.

"He made me help him unload the toys," Bert said.

"You mean the stolen toys?" said Flossie eagerly.

"No," said Bert. "A bunch of regular toys Mr. Jenkins was giving to the hospital."

"The *children's* ward?" asked Mr. Bobbsey.

Bert looked embarrassed. "Yes, sir."

Flossie wrapped her arms around her brother's neck. "Well, how did Bert know they were *old* new toys. I mean *new* old . . . I mean. Well, it's not his fault."

Their father began to chuckle softly.

Mrs. Bobbsey gave him a stern look. Then she turned to Bert. "Your father and I have to talk. We'll be right back."

After their parents closed the door, the kids looked at one another.

"I'm in for it now," Bert said.

"Yeah," said Freddie. "They'll probably ground you for life."

"Didn't you find anything at all?" Nan asked.

"No," Bert said. "Nothing that links the robbery to the fire. We've got to catch this crook soon. Before he steals or burns more of Mr. Jenkins's toys."

Nan leaned forward. "Freddie and I read Mom's notes."

"Old toys are sure worth a lot of money," said Freddie.

"We know that," Bert said. "What we don't know is who started the fire."

"And who knocked that display case on me," Freddie added.

"I still say it was Mr. Desmond," Flossie said. "He likes money more than anything. Just like Freddie."

"I do not! I— Oh, what's the use?" Freddie

flopped on his back and stared at the ceiling.

"I guess we should check out Mr. Desmond," said Bert.

Nan looked at her sketches of their suspects. For a moment she stared at the picture of Miss Penny holding her arm. Then she turned to her picture of Mr. Desmond. "Leave it to me and Flossie. We can go to his antiques shop early tomorrow morning."

"Not too early," said Flossie, patting her cheeks. "I need my beauty sleep." She had seen someone do that in a movie on TV.

"You sure do," Freddie said, laughing.

Flossie grabbed a pillow. She was just about to bean Freddie, when their parents appeared at the door.

"Uh-oh," Freddie whispered to Bert. "Here it comes."

"Bert," Mr. Bobbsey said quietly. "Your mother and I have decided that you will have laundry duty for the whole family—for the next two weeks."

Bert fell face down on his bed. "Oh, brother. Two whole weeks of Freddie's smelly socks," he groaned.

The next morning Nan and Flossie stood in front of Mr. Desmond's shop and warehouse. The sign on the window read: Seek Antiques—

Hubert Desmond, proprietor. The girls walked in.

They were impressed with what they saw inside. The shop was filled with beautiful old clocks, furniture, and toys.

Flossie looked at her hair in a gold-framed mirror. Meanwhile Nan spotted an open door leading to the storeroom in back of the shop. She was about to investigate, when the salesperson approached them.

"May I help you?" the lady asked in a friendly voice.

Nan nudged Flossie, and the younger Bobbsey said, "Yes, ma'am. We want to buy a present for our mom. It has to be *ever so perfect.*" Flossie put her head to one side and smiled up at the woman brightly.

Nan winced. She wondered what movie Flossie had taken this bit from. But the salesperson loved it and began showing Flossie around the shop.

Nan waited until they had moved away, then she went through the storeroom door.

The room was large and creepy-looking. There were tall stacks of boxes and crates, with narrow aisles in between. Only a few dimly lit lamps hung from the ceiling. And almost everywhere Nan looked there were long, dark shadows.

Nan knew she had to search quickly. Even Flossie couldn't talk forever.

Nan moved between the boxes. She kept hearing faint noises—thin, scratching sounds that scurried around her. Nan could feel her skin begin to crawl. She didn't want to think what things might be watching her.

As Nan turned a corner she spotted a work-table at the side of the room. "Just like the one Mr. Jenkins has," she whispered.

Nan passed cans of paint and large bags of cotton as she approached the table. When she reached it, Nan could see that it was covered with different types of toy parts: wagon wheels, doll's furniture, glass eyes, and pieces of fabric.

Nan heard the scratching sound again. She shivered, then forced herself to think about the things on the table. This had to be where Mr. Desmond made the fake fire wagon. Now all she had to do was find some real proof.

Again Nan heard a noise. It was closer this time. But it was a heavier sound than the one before. And it sounded as if it were right behind her.

Before Nan could turn around she was grabbed by two powerful hands.

"I've got you now," a raspy voice whispered. "I've got you!"

6

The Pieces Fit

The hands turned Nan around. It was Hubert Desmond. The angry antiques dealer stared into her eyes. "Just what do you think you're doing in here?"

At first Nan didn't know what to say. Then a plan flashed into her head. She had to get Mr. Desmond to admit in front of witnesses what he'd done. That was the only way to close the case and save the toy museum.

"I came here to prove something." Nan tried to sound confident.

"And what is that?" Mr. Desmond growled.

"That you're the one who took Mr. Jenkins's antique toy."

Mr. Desmond's face reddened. He let go of Nan and took a step back. But he still blocked her way out of the storeroom. "And why do you think *I* stole that toy from Tobias?"

"We figured it out. And these"—Nan pointed to the toy parts—"these prove that you're the one who made the fake toy. The one the crook left behind."

"Do they now?" Hubert Desmond took a step toward Nan. "Well, let me tell you—"

Before Mr. Desmond could finish his sentence, there was a loud scream.

"Leave my sister alone!"

Mr. Desmond turned around and saw Flossie running at him. Startled, the heavyset antiques dealer moved away. But he bumped into a shelf. An open can of paint toppled over onto him.

"My suit!" screamed the antiques dealer. "My most expensive suit!" He stood there in amazement as the paint dripped down his jacket.

Flossie ran up to her older sister just as the salesperson and several customers rushed in.

"Great!" Nan said to Flossie. "Now we'll have witnesses when we prove he's the crook."

"What is going on here?" asked the salesperson.

"We think Mr. Desmond is the Lakeport toy thief," Nan explained. She pointed to the toy parts and told how they figured in the case.

"We restore antique toys," Mr. Desmond said through gritted teeth. "We repair them for customers. Sometimes we have to repair a toy *before* we sell it. That's why those parts are here." Mr. Desmond grabbed a rag from the worktable. He gingerly tried to wipe some of the paint off. He only made it worse.

"That's true," said the salesperson. She picked up some of the parts. "And we always use the right parts for each toy. Metal wheels for carts and wagons. And glass eyes for dolls and stuffed animals. Why, Mr. Desmond's selection of antique toys is almost as large as Mr. Jenkins's."

The customers began staring at the Bobbsey girls. Nan's shoulders sagged. Her "evidence" had just gone up in smoke. And the customers thought she was just a silly kid.

"Why did you suspect me?" Hubert Desmond asked.

Flossie took a step forward. "Because you like money more than—"

Nan quickly covered Flossie's mouth and rushed them out of the storeroom. She'd been embarrassed enough for one morning.

Early that afternoon the four Bobbseys biked over to Jillian's house. The ride took them

through one of the prettiest areas in Lakeport. They rode past rolling hills, tree-lined streets, and large, beautiful mansions.

Flossie had spent most of the ride telling how she saved Nan.

Nan was grateful, but she really wanted to forget the whole thing. "We always use authentic parts. From metal to glass," Nan mimicked the salesperson. "And all those customers staring at me. I felt like a real jerk."

"Don't worry about it, Nan," Bert said. "All that matters is what we learned from this." Bert frowned. "What *did* we learn from this?"

"Nothing!" Nan exclaimed. "All I've proven is that Mr. Desmond isn't guilty."

"Yeah," said Bert. "If he wanted the toys for himself, why would he burn up the teddy bears?"

"Gee," Flossie said. She was a little out of breath. The hill they were on was very steep. "It's too bad we couldn't save those bears. The only things left were ashes."

The Bobbseys reached the top of the hill. The Jenkins mansion was just ahead of them.

"That's right," said Nan. "There wasn't a single thing—" Nan brought her bike to a sudden stop. "Everything burned!"

"We already know that, Nan." Bert pulled up next to her. "It's not the latest news flash."

Flossie joined Bert and Nan, and Freddie circled the threesome.

"Don't you get it?" Nan was excited. "If those had been authentic bears—they would've had glass eyes!"

"So?" asked Flossie.

Bert suddenly caught on. "Glass doesn't melt easily! We learned that in science class!"

"So glass eyes wouldn't have melted," Nan concluded. "That means the eyes were plastic, and—"

"The bears were fakes!" all the Bobbseys shouted at once.

"Someone stole the real bears and replaced them with fakes," Nan added. "Just like the fire wagon."

Bert did a wheelie on his bike. "Let's tell Mr. Jenkins quick!"

The kids rode up the steep driveway toward the house. They zipped past Mr. Jenkins's antique limo and stopped at the front door.

Bert leapt from his bike. He was just about to ring the bell, when the door flew open. Mr. Jenkins rushed out, calling for Jillian. He nearly knocked Bert down.

"I'm sorry, Bert," said the elderly toy man. "But I've just discovered that Jillian is gone!"

"Gone?" exclaimed Flossie and Freddie.

"Yes," said Mr. Jenkins. "She left a note saying she was running away. She didn't want to cause me any more trouble."

"We'll help find her, Mr. Jenkins," Nan offered. "Maybe she hasn't gone far. Bert and I will look around back. You and Flossie can look in the house. Just in case she's hiding there. And Freddie"—she turned to her younger brother—"you check the street."

Everyone rushed off.

Freddie whipped his bike around and started down the driveway. But as he passed Mr. Jenkins's car he thought he saw something move inside.

Freddie parked his bike. Then he slowly crept up on the car. When he reached the passenger door, he jumped up, shouting, "All right, freeze!"

He looked inside the car. Jillian was huddled down next to the steering wheel. She scrambled out the driver's side and began running down the driveway.

Freddie bolted after Jillian and caught her. "Why are you running away?" he asked.

"Because I'm a jinx!" Jillian shouted. "I'm even bad luck to Grandpa!" She began sobbing.

Freddie shoved his hands into his pockets. "You're not a jinx, Jillian. Honest. We've just found out something."

"Really?" Jillian asked.

"We sure have!" said Freddie. "You wait. Things'll be fine. We'll find the real crooks. I promise."

The two of them stood there talking. Neither heard the sound of gears grinding as the large black car slipped out of the park position.

The car began to roll down the steep, narrow driveway.

In a few seconds the huge limo was heading straight for the children. And there was no one around to stop it!

7

Model for Danger

"Freddie, look out!" The cry came from Bert Bobbsey as he and Nan raced across the front lawn.

Freddie turned in time to see the car barreling down the driveway toward them. He grabbed Jillian and dove out of the way just as it rolled by.

Nan ran up to them as Bert raced after the limo.

When he caught up to the car, he jumped onto the running board on the driver's side. Reaching inside, he pulled the parking brake as hard as he could. The car stopped only a few feet from the top of a hill.

The other Bobbseys, Jillian, and Mr. Jenkins ran to the car.

"Are you all right?" Flossie asked.

"Sure." Bert's answer was short as he gasped for breath. He'd just done a dangerous thing—and he knew it.

"Why did you do that?" asked Mr. Jenkins. He leaned into the car and double-checked the brakes. "The kids were out of danger."

Bert pointed to the bottom of the hill. Mr. Jenkins looked down and saw several children riding around on their bikes.

"We passed them on our way here," Bert said. He dropped down on the running board. Freddie sat next to him, and Bert ruffled his hair.

Mr. Jenkins took Jillian in his arms. "Don't worry, sweetheart. It's really not your fault." He hugged her gently.

Nan didn't want to interrupt, but she had to. "Mr. Jenkins. We've discovered something that won't make you happy."

Ten minutes later the Bobbseys had explained all about the teddy bears and the fire. Nan could tell that the news had really upset Mr. Jenkins. For the first time the toy man looked angry.

"This is terrible," said Mr. Jenkins. "I should have noticed that myself."

"That's all right, Grandpa." Jillian took his hand.

"Not really, sweetheart," Mr. Jenkins said. "If there are any more fake toys, it could ruin everything. No one will come to a museum filled with fakes. I'd better get over there. I need to check every exhibit before the opening tomorrow."

"I'll go with you," Jillian said.

Mr. Jenkins turned to the Bobbseys. "Thank you, children. You've helped me more than I can say. I'll call Miss Penny and have her meet me at the museum." With that, he slipped into the car and returned it to the driveway.

The Bobbseys watched Mr. Jenkins and Jillian hurry into the house. After the front door closed, the twins walked back to their bikes.

"Now what do we do?" asked Freddie.

"We've got to find out who wants to wreck Mr. Jenkins's museum." Bert picked up his bike and swung onto the seat.

Flossie looked angry. "Who'd want to keep us kids from seeing all those great old toys?"

"Maybe it's one of the other toy-store owners," said Freddie. "Maybe they're jealous."

"Why?" asked Flossie.

"Because so many kids go to More and More Toys." Freddie hoped Nan or Bert would agree with him.

"I don't think so," said Nan. "But maybe the crook bought the fake toys from another toy store."

"And one of the store owners might remember something." Bert leaned forward over the handlebars. "Let's check it out!"

"Okay," said Nan. "I'll take the west side of town. Bert and Freddie can take the east side. And Flossie—"

"I know." Flossie headed for the front door of the Jenkins house. "Keep an eye on Jillian and Mr. Jenkins."

"Thanks, Floss." Nan smiled. "We'll pick you up later, at the museum."

Flossie entered the Jenkins mansion as the other Bobbseys sped off down the hill.

For the next two hours Bert and Freddie rode all around Lakeport's shopping area. They questioned every toy-store owner they could find. Did they sell antique bears or fire wagons? Had anyone bought any toys that looked like the ones stolen from Mr. Jenkins? Had the store owners seen anything that looked suspicious?

The answer they got was the same from everybody—no. No one seemed to know anything.

On the west side of town Nan wasn't doing any better. She was pretty disappointed as she left a toy store near the wharves.

Nan walked across the street to the docks. She chained her bike to a post and walked along the pier.

For a while Nan just stared at the sunlight flickering on the water. Then something else caught her eye. Something in the sky. A small shape was flying out of the sun, heading in her direction.

At first Nan thought it was a bird. But as it got closer she noticed it was a remote-controlled plane. She could hear the engine and see its whirling propeller.

Nan quickly looked around to see who was working it, but there wasn't anyone in sight.

She looked up again. The plane was flying lower now. Nan suddenly realized that it wasn't going to land on the pier. It was diving at her!

Nan ducked just in time. The plane zoomed by, inches from her head. She could feel the rush of air along the back of her neck.

The plane did a loop and headed back toward Nan.

Nan began running away from the plane. She could hear the angry growl of its engine.

The plane was getting closer and closer. At the last moment Nan dropped to the ground. The plane swooped over her head. Then it made a sharp turn. It was coming back.

Nan turned to run, but there was nowhere to go.

She'd reached the end of the wharf. To her left and to her right were the icy cold waters of the lake.

Nan was trapped.

8

A Huggable Clue

Nan frantically searched for a way out. The plane was closing in fast. Then an idea came to her. She spotted a fishing net covering one of the dock posts.

Nan grabbed the net and swung at the plane with all her strength. She knocked the robot plane off course. A second later it crashed into the water—and sank.

Nan slowly rose to her feet and looked around. She still couldn't see who had been working the plane. Then she heard a car racing away from the other end of the pier. The sound of screeching tires faded in the distance.

Now I know someone wants us off this case, Nan thought to herself. Well—fat chance.

"Attacked by a toy!" Bert Bobbsey was angry. "I don't believe this!"

Nan sat at the kitchen table doodling on her sketch pad. "Look, I got away, didn't I?"

"Sure," said Freddie. He was pouring chocolate syrup into an empty glass. "But you could have been hurt."

"I don't think so," said Nan. "I think someone was only trying to scare me."

"So what do we do now?" Flossie asked.

"I don't know," Nan said. She looked over at Freddie, who was still pouring syrup into his glass. "Don't you want some milk with that syrup?"

Freddie grinned. "Maybe just a little."

"I say we follow Rex Sleuther's rule number nineteen," Bert said. "Always check in with the local crime-stoppers."

"Who?" said Freddie as he finally poured milk into his glass.

"The police," Bert said. "We go see Lieutenant Pike."

"He won't tell us anything," said Nan.

"Yes, he will," Bert said, smiling, "if Flossie does the asking. How about it, Flossie?"

"Oh." Flossie sighed. "If I have to." She grinned at Nan.

They waited until Freddie had downed his glass of chocolate milk. Then they all headed out the door.

All the officers on the Lakeport police force knew the Bobbsey twins, so they weren't surprised when the kids walked into the squad room. Even Lieutenant Pike almost smiled when he saw them. Almost.

"Hi, Lieutenant Pike," said Flossie. She rested her chin on his desk. "We came to see how you were doing."

The lieutenant nodded to the kids. "I'm sure you did. You also want to know how the case is coming along. Right?"

Flossie looked up at Bert. "I told you he was the smartest detective in the *whole* police force. Didn't I?"

Nan rolled her eyes. She had to have a talk with her little sister. Flossie was definitely watching too many movies.

"Look," Lieutenant Pike said. "You know I like you. You're good kids. And you care about people." The detective rubbed his forehead. "But I'm the one with the badge.

"Police work can be hard and dangerous. Right?" The Bobbseys nodded in agreement. "Right! Now, I want you to be *concerned citizens.* But please—leave the police work to me. Okay?"

"Okay," the Bobbseys said together.

There was a moment of silence. Then Flossie spoke up. "Lieutenant Pike, have you found *all* the missing toys yet?"

"Now, Flossie, what did I just—" The policeman looked puzzled. "What do you mean—all the toys? Only one toy is missing."

The Bobbseys calmly told the lieutenant what they had discovered. And how they were sure someone was stealing Mr. Jenkins's toy collection.

Lieutenant Pike leaned back in his chair and sighed. "Wonderful. We haven't even found where a crook could sell this stuff."

"They'd sell the toys to a *fence*," Bert said.

"A wooden fence or a wire fence?" asked Flossie.

"No, Flossie," Nan said. "*Fence* is a police word. It means someone who buys stolen things. Then he sells them to other people."

"Exactly," Lieutenant Pike agreed. "If a thief took these toys, then he'd have to sell them to someone."

"Yeah," said Bert. "And the more toys he steals, the more money he makes. But how did he know which toys to steal?"

"And how will he get them out of town?" asked Nan.

"How does he know how much they're worth?" Freddie added.

Lieutenant Pike stared at the Bobbseys.

"Kids, I'm afraid I'll have to ask you to leave now. I—I have a lot of work to do."

"Oh, sure, Lieutenant Pike." Nan began leading Freddie and Flossie away from his desk. "We'll come back some other time."

"I'm sure you will," said the lieutenant. "And thanks for the new information."

"No problem," Bert said, backing away from the desk. "We were just being—concerned citizens."

Bert turned around and ran to catch up with the others.

The Bobbseys were excited as they left the station. They began exchanging ideas as they headed for the bike racks.

"This is great!" Bert cheered. "We learned something that time!"

"Right," said Nan eagerly. "Now we know that the thief has to have a way to sell the toys. Just like stolen jewelry."

Nan, Bert, and Freddie reached their bikes first. They began unlocking them from the rack as Flossie approached her bike.

"I still think the crook owns a toy store," said Freddie. "He's someone who's jealous of Mr. Jenkins."

"Well, I think—" Flossie stopped in midsentence. She was staring at a package in her bike basket. It was large and wrapped in brown paper. "What's this?" she said.

The Bobbseys looked at one another. Then Bert picked up the bundle and tore it open. Inside was a talking toy. It was in the shape of a smiling stuffed donkey.

"It's Loudmouth Lou!" Flossie squealed. She grabbed the cuddly animal. "You push the button and he says funny things."

Flossie reached in back and pushed the button. The donkey's eyes blinked, and its mouth began opening and closing. But the message they heard wasn't funny at all. In a piercing, witchlike voice the toy said:

> Little girls and little boys
> Shouldn't play with grown-up toys
> I see you now, I'm watching you
> Stay off the case, or else—
> Boo-hoo!

The frightening rhyme was followed by a string of terrible witch's cackles. Then silence.

9

Back to Toyland

Nan took the doll from Flossie. "Should we show this to Lieutenant Pike?"

"I don't think so," Bert replied. "He'll show it to our parents—"

"And they'll get all worried about us," Freddie cut in. "They don't know we can handle any crook."

"The museum opens tomorrow," Bert continued. "We don't have much time."

"Well, I think this crook is really rotten," Flossie said angrily. "He's stealing toys. And he's using toys to scare us." She folded her arms and sat down next to her bike.

"You're right, Floss," said Nan. "This whole

mystery has been about toys. Even the warn-
ings."

"I'll say. The crook almost knocked over a
toy case on me," Freddie grumbled.

"That was probably an accident, Freddie,"
said Bert. "He bumped into it trying to run
away."

"That must have hurt his arms," Nan said.
She stared at Flossie. Suddenly Nan exclaimed,
"Wait a minute! What if we've been after the
wrong person?"

"Which wrong person?" asked Bert.

"What if it isn't Mr. Desmond?" Nan replied. "What if the crook is Miss Penny?"

Nan grabbed her sketch pad from her bike
rack. She quickly turned the pages until she
found her picture of Miss Penny. "See? This is
her in Mr. Jenkins's office. She was always
holding her arms like this. Just like Flossie is
doing."

"You mean she was really holding her arms
because they hurt!" Bert exclaimed.

"She was the one who knocked the case
over?" Freddie looked totally amazed.

"I just remembered something else," Nan
said. "At the toy store Miss Penny told Mr.
Jenkins that she hadn't seen the fire wagon or
the doll. Remember?"

"Yeah . . ." said Bert hesitantly. "She said she
hadn't been in his workshop that day."

"Right," Nan agreed. "But after the display case fell over, she said the fire wagon had been on the top shelf. How did she know that?"

"Yeah!" Bert exclaimed.

"But where did she put the real fire wagon?" Freddie asked.

"I don't know yet," said Nan. "But we'd better find out by tomorrow. Or the Lakeport Toy Museum may never open."

The Bobbseys were up very early Saturday morning. They were worried. They still didn't know where the real fire wagon or teddy bears were hidden.

After a quick breakfast they biked over to the Jenkins house.

When they arrived, Jillian led them into the living room to see her grandfather.

Tobias Jenkins looked tired. "Miss Penny and I were at the museum from the afternoon until very late last night. We checked over half of the antique toys. We discovered that many of them had been replaced by fakes. I've called Lieutenant Pike about it, and I've called all the people that sold me the toys. No one seemed to know anything."

"Will you open the museum today?" Flossie asked anxiously.

"I don't know," Mr. Jenkins said sadly.

"Without the real antique toys, there's no reason for the museum to open. No reason at all."

The Bobbseys exchanged glances. They knew they had to find the missing toys *soon*.

Nan was confused. "Miss Penny was with Mr. Jenkins yesterday afternoon and evening," she whispered to Bert.

"That's what he said," Bert replied.

"Then how could she leave the message in the toy?" Nan asked.

Bert looked at his sister. "Good question."

"Where is Miss Penny now?" Nan asked Mr. Jenkins.

"I believe she's at the store," said Mr. Jenkins. "It's closed this morning. I think she wanted to count some of the store's merchandise. We're having a special sale next week."

Bert suddenly started pushing the other Bobbseys out of the room. "We'll go help her, Mr. Jenkins. And don't worry. Everything will be just fine."

"Wait!" Jillian shouted. "I'm going with you. Can I, Grandpa?"

Her grandfather gave his permission, and the kids rushed from the room.

Outside, Bert hustled everybody onto their bikes. Soon they were pedaling toward the store. Bert and Nan were in the lead. Flossie, Freddie, and Jillian followed behind them.

"What's going on, Bert?" Nan shouted.

"Remember where you hid your diary that time I wanted to read it?"

"Sure," Nan answered. "In the living room with a bunch of books. That way nobody would notice it."

Bert smiled. "And where would you hide a stolen toy?"

Nan's eyes widened. "With a bunch of other toys!" she shouted. "The toy store! They're in the toy store!"

By the time the kids reached the store, Freddie had told Jillian everything. She couldn't believe Miss Penny would steal, but she agreed to let the Bobbseys handle things.

The problem was that they didn't have a plan. They just knew that somehow they had to search the store. They had to find the stolen toys.

The kids went to the side door and rang the bell.

Celia Penny was surprised when she opened the door and five children rushed inside.

"Hello, Miss Penny," said Nan. "Mr. Jenkins sent us to help you."

"I really don't need any help, thank you," Miss Penny said.

"That's okay," said Flossie. She ran farther

into the store. "We'll just look around." Freddie and Jillian ran after her. And Miss Penny chased after them.

"Keep her busy," Bert whispered to Nan. "I've got an idea." He began backing toward the door.

Nan nodded, then joined the other kids.

Meanwhile Bert pulled a piece of tape off a nearby dispenser. He managed to place the tape over the door latch just in time. The tape would keep the door unlocked.

Miss Penny was ushering the kids back toward the door. "I really do appreciate your offer. But I don't need help right now."

Nan looked at Bert. He signaled her that everything was set. Then Nan got an idea of her own.

"That's okay," Nan said cheerfully. "We have to go see Lieutenant Pike anyway."

Miss Penny became very nervous. "Why is that?"

"Somebody sent us a doll with a nasty message in it. We gave it to the police this morning. And they found fingerprints."

"Yeah," said Bert. He had caught on to Nan's plan. "They'll know who the crook is real soon."

"And they'll know what kind of *fence* he has too," Flossie added.

Miss Penny opened the door and waved them outside. "Well . . . uh, that's wonderful. Uh, thank you for coming." And she slammed the door shut.

Bert signaled everyone to be quiet. He listened at the door for a few minutes. Then, when he thought it was safe, he pulled it open.

The children quietly tiptoed back inside.

They entered the main part of the store and headed for the back area.

As they were approaching Miss Penny's office, the door opened. The kids silently dropped to the floor just in time. They watched as Miss Penny hurried from her office. She went down an aisle and through a door marked Basement.

"Come on," said Bert. "We can't lose her now. Sleuther's rule num—"

Nan put her hand over his mouth. "Not now, Bert. Not now."

The children hurried down the aisle and quietly slipped through the door. They moved cautiously down the dimly lit stairwell.

They quietly searched through the basement until Bert and Nan signaled for everyone to stop. Celia Penny was in a small storeroom just a few feet ahead of them.

"That's where we keep all the broken toys," Jillian whispered to the Bobbseys. "When

Grandpa can't fix them, he sends them back."

"And I bet that's where she got the parts she needed." Nan suddenly pointed at the store manager. "Look!"

Miss Penny had pulled a teddy bear out of one of the boxes.

"That looks like one of Grandpa's bears!" Jillian exclaimed. "The bears that were burned in the fire."

"That's our evidence!" Freddie jumped up and rushed into the room. "All right, Miss Penny! Drop that bear!"

A startled Miss Penny stepped back as the other children rushed into the room. Freddie began accusing her of being the Lakeport toy thief.

But Nan was uneasy. "We should have gone for the police," Nan whispered to Bert. "I don't like this."

"What do you mean?" Bert asked.

"I still don't know how she could have sent us that talking toy. She was with Mr. Jenkins at the museum."

"Well," Bert said. "Let's ask her."

Bert stepped toward Miss Penny. "How'd you send us that warning in the donkey? And where'd you get the parts to make the fake toys?"

"Why, I gave them to her," a voice declared from behind the children.

They all turned to see Hubert Desmond blocking the door.

"And now, little boys and girls"—Desmond's mouth curled into a wicked smile—"it's boo-hoo time."

10

Wrap 'Em Up

"What are we going to do?" Miss Penny asked. "They know everything!"

"Don't worry, Celia," the heavyset antiques dealer said as he took some rope off a wall rack. "We'll simply tie them up and leave them here. Then we'll make our getaway. The store is closed until Monday—thanks to dear old Tobias."

"But he knows they're here! And the police! They have your fingerprints!" Miss Penny looked around nervously.

Mr. Desmond chuckled. "Celia, I wore gloves when I delivered that toy donkey. There *were* no prints."

"Did you wear gloves when you flew the model plane?" Nan asked.

"Naturally. And when I set the museum fire. I'm a very careful man."

While Mr. Desmond was talking, Bert spotted the light switch. It was on the wall next to Nan. He had an idea. Now, if he could only get Nan's attention.

"How could you do this to Grandpa?" Jillian's eyes were filled with anger.

"This toy museum would have made Tobias's collection famous," Hubert Desmond snarled. "Much more famous than mine. I couldn't let that happen. Besides . . . your grandfather's antique toys are worth a lot of money. After I sell them, I'll be very, very rich."

"So it was you who switched fake toys for the real ones," said Bert.

"Exactly." Mr. Desmond smiled wickedly. "It would have made Tobias look like a fool. A collection of fakes!"

Suddenly Mr. Desmond grabbed Bert and started to tie his hands together. "I suggest none of you move. You'll be found soon enough."

"What are you going to do?" Bert struggled a little. He was really trying to signal Nan. He had to get her to notice the light switch. "Are you going to leave us here—*in the dark.*" Bert shifted his eyes from Nan to the wall switch.

Nan caught on. She spotted the switch and knew what to do.

"Yes." Hubert Desmond chuckled. "In the dark."

"You can't do that," Nan pleaded. "My little sister is afraid of the dark. Aren't you, Flossie?"

Flossie wasn't sure what was happening. She looked confused. Even a little frightened.

"Yes," Nan continued. "She really gets scared. She even starts to *panic.*" For a minute Nan wasn't sure if Flossie was going to catch on.

Then suddenly Flossie exploded into a wild screaming frenzy. She started running around the tiny room. "Don't leave me in the dark! I'm afraid of ghosts!"

Mr. Desmond and Miss Penny were caught off guard. At that instant Nan hit the light switch and the room went black.

"Run!" Nan shouted.

The five children bolted from the room, slamming the door behind them.

They could hear the adults stumbling around and bumping into things.

Ducking behind some boxes, Nan quickly untied Bert.

"Let's go get the police!" Bert said.

The kids started upstairs. They could hear Mr. Desmond and Miss Penny running through the basement.

"Don't let them g[...]" shouted Mr. Desmond.

The Bobbseys and Jillian [...] main floor and hid among the toys.

"If we go for the police, they'll get away," said Bert.

"Then we'll have to send Freddie, Flossie, and Jillian." Nan turned to them. "You guys have to do it. Bert and I will try to stall them until you get back."

"But—" Freddie tried to protest.

"No buts, Freddie," said Bert. "Go!"

Bert and Nan moved swiftly along the aisles. When they were far enough from the others, they started yelling to get the crooks' attention.

"There they are!" Celia Penny called out.

Freddie, Flossie, and Jillian hid behind a display as the two crooks ran by them.

Then Jillian led the younger Bobbseys down the aisles. Soon they were sneaking through the exit door.

"We can't do it!" said Flossie once they were outside. "We can't leave Bert and Nan in there all alone."

"Flossie is right," Freddie said. "Jillian, *you* have to go for the police!"

"But what if I can't find them?" Jillian looked up and down the empty street. "What if I jinx us all and—"

"You're not a jinx, Jillian!" Freddie rolled his

it was dumb for me to call you that! *I'm* dumb. Okay."

"He *is,* Jillian." Flossie added urgently. "Now, go get help!" She and Freddie turned and ran back into the store.

Once inside, Flossie and Freddie crept back into the main room. They spotted Bert and Nan huddled behind a rack of baseball uniforms.

"What are you doing back here?" Nan whispered as Flossie and Freddie joined them.

"Catching a couple of crooks. What else?" Freddie smiled. He quickly explained that Jillian had gone for help.

"Okay then," said Bert. "Let's get 'em."

The Bobbseys took off down the aisles.

When they reached the center of the store, they started screaming. They wanted the crooks to chase them.

"There they are!" Hubert Desmond shouted.

Suddenly the kids split up. They ran up and down the aisles, dodging the crooks at every turn.

To confuse the crooks, Nan and Freddie turned on every talking display they could find. They switched on all the portable radios and tape players. The store was filled with the loud squawking and music of the toys. Flossie sprayed Fun Foam on the floor. She watched Miss Penny slip on it and slide into a display of

Creepy Goo Monsters. The store manager was covered with slimy green foam.

Meanwhile Bert was being chased by Hubert Desmond. But the heavyset man was running out of breath. Several times he thought he had Bert. But Bert would slide under a table or climb over the shelves.

And then, over the noise, they all heard police sirens.

"Let's get out of here!" Mr. Desmond shouted. He grabbed Miss Penny's arm and tried to rush her out. But as they turned a corner they stopped cold.

Freddie was driving toward them in a miniature car. From another direction Nan sprayed them with Party String.

The two began backing up. Suddenly a creature with flashing green eyes and wild red hair came running toward Hubert Desmond. The creature roared as it raised its huge, hairy hands.

Hubert Desmond jumped back and fell into a wading pool full of water.

The creature removed its rubber mask and monster gloves. There stood Flossie, smiling from ear to ear.

Freddie zoomed past Celia Penny, causing her to fall into a baby carriage.

Bert and Nan quickly threw a large fishing net over her—just as Jillian rushed in with Lieu-

tenant Pike. They were followed by two police officers.

"Hi, Lieutenant Pike." Flossie beamed at him.

Lieutenant Pike looked at the two messy criminals, then at the four children. "I don't believe it," he muttered softly. "I really don't believe it."

Nan and Bert were leaning against each other.

"Just being *concerned citizens*," Nan said, smiling.

Bert pulled up his collar. "Looks like this case is closed."

There was a large crowd inside the toy museum. Kids and grown-ups were having a wonderful time. They looked at stuffed animals and electric trains. They watched mechanical monkeys climbing and dollhouses lighting up.

Music boxes played, and wind-up toys jumped and tumbled. Even toy steamboats puffed smoke from their stacks.

Tobias Jenkins was happy. He and Jillian stood in the main hall with the whole Bobbsey family.

"I can't thank you enough," he said to the twins and their parents. "This is just what I wanted to see."

"We're glad it all worked out," said Mrs. Bobbsey. "The police even found all your stolen toys."

"Yeah," said Bert. "The crooks had them hidden in your own store."

"I knew it was Mr. Desmond all the time," said Flossie. "He paid Miss Penny a lot of money to steal your collection."

"That's true," Mr. Jenkins said. "He needed her to steal the toys before they were moved to the museum. He knew that once they were in here, he wouldn't be able to get to them."

"But we discovered the fake fire wagon and spoiled his plan," Nan added.

"Right," said Bert.

Mrs. Bobbsey chuckled. "When you children discovered the fakes, Mr. Desmond and Miss Penny tried to destroy them. They were evidence."

"That's why they set fire to the teddy bears," said Flossie.

Tobias Jenkins sighed. "To think they almost got away with it."

Bert tucked his thumbs in his belt. "Well, crooks always make one big mistake."

"I agree," said Tobias Jenkins. His eyes twinkled. "And Hubert Desmond's big mistake was trying his thievery in Lakeport—the headquarters for the Bobbsey twins!"